The ONCE UPON AMERICA ® Series

A LONG WAY TO GO
A Story of Women's Right to Vote

HERO OVER HERE
A Story of World War I

IT'S ONLY GOODBYE
An Immigrant Story

THE DAY IT RAINED FOREVER
A Story of the Johnstown Flood

PEARL HARBOR IS BURNING!
A Story of World War II

CHILD STAR
When Talkies Came to Hollywood

THE BITE OF THE GOLD BUG
A Story of the Alaskan Gold Rush

FIRE!
The Beginnings of the Labor Movement

NIGHT BIRD
A Story of the Seminole Indians

CLOSE TO HOME
A Story of the Polio Epidemic

HARD TIMES
A Story of the Great Depression

EARTHQUAKE!
A Story of Old San Francisco

Hard Times

A STORY OF THE GREAT DEPRESSION

BY NANCY ANTLE

ILLUSTRATED BY JAMES WATLING

VIKING

Thanks to James Thearl Antle, Rosa Lea Antle, and Evelyn Antle for sharing their memories with me. And to Rick, for his help on the last two pages—I couldn't have done it without you.

VIKING
Published by the Penguin Group
Penguin Books USA Inc., 375 Hudson Street, New York, New York 10014, U.S.A.
Penguin Books Ltd, 27 Wrights Lane, London W8 5TZ, England
Penguin Books Australia Ltd, Ringwood, Victoria, Australia
Penguin Books Canada Ltd, 10 Alcorn Avenue, Toronto, Ontario, Canada M4V 3B2
Penguin Books (N.Z.) Ltd, 182–190 Wairau Road, Auckland 10, New Zealand

Penguin Books Ltd, Registered Offices: Harmondsworth, Middlesex, England

First published in 1993 by Viking, a division of Penguin Books USA Inc.

1   3   5   7   9   10   8   6   4   2

Text copyright © Nancy Antle, 1993
Illustrations copyright © James Watling, 1993
All rights reserved

ONCE UPON AMERICA® is a registered trademark of Viking Penguin,
a division of Penguin Books USA Inc.

Library of Congress Cataloging-in-Publication Data
Antle, Nancy.
Hard times: a story of the Great Depression / by Nancy Antle:
illustrated by James Watling.   p.   cm.—(Once upon America)
Summary: In 1933, when drought and the Depression lay waste
to their native Oklahoma, fifth grader Charlie and his family
are forced to leave their home and search for a new way of life.
ISBN 0-670-84665-1
[1. Depressions—1929—Fiction.   2. Oklahoma—Fiction.]
I. Watling, James, ill.   II. Title.   III. Series.
PZ7.A6294Har   1993   [Fic]—dc20   92-41522   CIP   AC

Printed in U.S.A.

Set in 12 pt. Goudy Old Style

To Richard A. Thompson—
historian, anthropologist, archaeologist—
who gave me a love of finding out about the past.
Thanks, Dad.

Luck Runs Out

"I can't believe they're going to close the school. It's only March," Charlie's sister, Alma, said. She snapped another green bean in two. She threw it into a pot her mother was stirring.

"Don't make such a fuss," Charlie said. "You don't like school. You just want to see the boys." Alma was almost 15 and seemed to think of little else.

She ignored him, but her face turned red.

"Next year," Mama said, "you'll go to school in the city. You can ride in with Daddy."

Charlie took his harmonica from his overalls pocket. He polished its shiny surface with a corner of the kitchen tablecloth. The last place he wanted to be on a sunny day, or a rainy day for that matter, was school. He'd much rather take a walk and play his music.

"Did your teacher think they'd open again before summer?" Mama asked.

"Nope," Charlie said. Then he quoted his fifth grade teacher. "They haven't got money to pay the teachers or buy supplies."

Mama shook her head. "I guess their luck just ran out," she said.

"Like Lee," Alma said.

Charlie nodded. Lee was their older sister's husband. He had been laid off down at the railroad yard. His luck had run out.

Lee and Sally and their new baby, Roy, had moved home because they couldn't pay rent anymore. Charlie hadn't minded giving up his room for them. Sally was his favorite sister and he loved Roy. Besides, they said that next year Lee would get his job back and they could move out. But it was next year now. Roy was already walking and talking. Charlie still had to share a room with stupid old Alma.

Charlie didn't understand much about why people were losing their jobs. There had always been hard times in Oklahoma. Really hard times started four years ago, in 1929, when the stock market crashed. Whatever that meant. Charlie imagined giant buildings in New York City toppling over, one after another, like the dominoes he liked to set up on the living room floor.

A sudden gust of wind rattled the kitchen windows. A puff of dust blew in under the back door.

"Someone forgot to put the towel under the door again," Mama said, without looking up from the stove.

Charlie got up and stuffed the dish towel under the door. He *did* understand about the dust. There hadn't been enough rain in Oklahoma in a long time. The farmer's couldn't grow crops to sell, so they didn't have any money to pay their bills. Many of them were giving up and driving off to California to find jobs. Charlie saw their old trucks and cars drive by every day on the highway.

"When will Daddy get here?" Charlie asked. "I'm starving."

Mama looked at her watch. "He'll be here soon," she said. "He's usually home by now."

Daddy had been lucky so far. He had kept his job. It was true that they cut his hours. Fewer hours meant less money in Daddy's paycheck. Later they cut his hourly wage, so there was even less money every month. But he still had his job, fixing typewriters. Charlie heard Daddy say more than once, "I've been lucky so far because nobody can afford new typewriters." There were lots of old typewriters in the city.

"Set the table," Alma said. She set a stack of plates down hard on the table. The silverware on top jingled.

"It ain't my turn," Charlie said.

"It *isn't*," Mama corrected.

"Thank you for taking my side," Charlie said, grinning.

Mama didn't turn around from the stove, but he could tell she was smiling.

"Set the table, Charlie Boy," she said.

Charlie sighed. He laid the plates on the stained flowered tablecloth. When he was done, he got a spoon and tin cup out for Roy. He set them on the metal tray of Roy's highchair. It would be noisy, but Charlie liked to let Roy beat on the tray while he played his harmonica after dinner. Roy loved it.

The roar of an engine in need of a muffler filled the kitchen. Charlie slammed out the back door. Lee, Sally, Roy, and Daddy tumbled out of the pickup.

"Hey, Roy!" Charlie said. He lifted Roy up and swung him around in the soft dusty driveway. Roy's blond curls were matted with sweat. He had chocolate all over his mouth. Charlie thought he was adorable.

"Charlie, Charlie!" Roy shouted. "We move!"

Charlie stopped. "What?" He hoped he hadn't heard right.

Charlie's stomach felt tight.

"You'd better come inside, son," Daddy said. "We've got some things to talk over."

4

Inside, Daddy and Lee took off their hats and sat down at the table. Charlie put Roy in his highchair.

"Moving where?" Charlie asked Lee.

Lee looked at Sally and Daddy and then back at Charlie.

"Sally and me and Roy are moving to California," Lee said. "There's plenty of work there."

"Oh, Sally, you're too young to be going so far from home," Mama said. "You and Roy can stay here, at least."

"Mama, I'm seventeen and I've got a family of my own now," Sally said. "We've got to stick together."

This couldn't be happening, Charlie thought. He watched as the green beans boiled over on the stove. No one got up to turn down the fire.

"We're going to move, too," Daddy said.

Charlie felt better for a moment. They could go to California, too! Then all his hopes were slapped away.

"We'll be moving in with Grandma and Grandpa Dodson," he said. "I haven't been able to pay the mortgage on this house for over a year. And, today . . ." His voice trailed off.

Mama reached across the table to take his hand.

"Today my luck ran out," he said. "I got laid off."

No Tears

"Play me a song, Charlie," Mama said. "It'll sound real pretty in this empty old house."

Charlie sat on the kitchen floor, with his back against the wall. He took out his harmonica and polished it on his shirttail. His mother took another glass from the kitchen drainboard. She wrapped it in newspaper and put it into a wooden crate.

"I'll play if you'll sing," Charlie said. He thought Mama had the prettiest voice in Oklahoma.

"I don't feel much like singing."

"Please, Mama."

She smiled weakly and nodded. Charlie played a few notes. He knew she would want to sing a hymn. He chose "Amazing Grace" and began.

Mama's clear, sweet voice echoed off the walls, sounding ghostly in the bare house. Not even a curtain was left to catch the sound. Everything but the glasses had been packed into the truck and a little trailer.

Halfway through the second verse, Alma slammed the back door. Her eyes were red. She sat down on the floor beside Charlie. She had been to say good-bye to her best friend, Loretta.

"Keep singing," Alma said.

Charlie started again. They finished "Amazing Grace" and moved on to "Rock of Ages." Alma joined in on the second verse. Then she got up to help Mama pack glasses.

"I have a new song," Charlie said. "Heard it in town last Saturday."

"Where?" Alma asked.

"Were you listening to those hobos singing for dimes, after I told you not to?" Mama asked, frowning.

"They can't help it if they are out of work," Charlie said.

"That's true for most of them, I know. But some of those men have always been out of work. They are just plain crazy. You stay away from them."

"It's a great song, though," Charlie said.

Mama smiled.

"What is it called?" Alma asked. She reached for another piece of newspaper.

" 'Going Down the Road Feeling Bad,' " Charlie said.

Mama laughed, but not like she meant it.

"Save that one for our trip," she said. She looked over at Alma, whose eyes had gotten wide. She was staring at the newspaper she was holding.

"Goodness, Alma, what's wrong?" Mama asked.

Alma silently handed the paper to her mother.

"What?" Charlie asked.

" 'A father of four who lost his fortune in the Crash of '29 said he couldn't take it anymore,' " Mama read out loud. " 'He jumped to his death from the First National Bank Building.' "

"I went to school with his daughter," Alma said, staring straight ahead. "She had such beautiful clothes. I was jealous. I wanted to be just like her."

Charlie heard about people killing themselves in New York City when the Crash came. But that was miles away and a long time ago. Things like that didn't happen in Oklahoma City. They couldn't.

The truck rumbled into the driveway beside the house. Daddy came in, jingling his keys. He carried a brown paper bag.

"I brought us a treat," he said. "What's wrong with everyone?"

10

It wasn't right, Charlie thought, looking at Daddy. Fathers shouldn't one day just kill themselves and leave you on your own. Parents were supposed to take care of you.

Daddy raised his eyebrows at Mama, silently asking a question.

"Someone Alma knew," Mama said. "Her father killed himself yesterday."

"I saw it happen," Daddy said.

"Oh, Lord," Mama said, putting her hand over her heart.

"I was in town getting my things from work." Daddy rubbed his eyes with both hands.

"People tried to stop him. He kept saying he was a terrible father since he didn't have any money."

"Didn't he know his family needed him—not money?" Alma asked. Daddy put an arm around her.

"I guess he didn't understand, sweetheart," Daddy said. "Sometimes people that have been poor and get rich can't stand being poor again."

Charlie stood up and Daddy put his other arm around him.

"Luckily, we've never been rich. Right, Mama?"

Mama smiled. Daddy reached inside the bag. He brought out cold bottles of Coca-Cola.

Daddy held the cold bottle by his face.

"Don't wear a tired, thirsty face," Daddy said, smiling. Charlie laughed. Roy had repeated the Coca-Cola slogan at least a hundred times. For a while, they had all been sorry Roy had learned to talk.

The others opened their pop. They sat on the floor drinking it in the quiet house. Charlie didn't feel much like drinking anything right now. He decided to save his for the trip.

"Charlie, take the dust mop and go over the floors real quick," Mama said.

He nodded. He played his harmonica with one hand and pushed the mop with the other. It was just like Mama to insist on a clean house. It didn't matter that the next people to see it were going to be the bank people. The people who were making them move.

Just as he finished the floors, he heard Roy running into the empty house. He had been to say good-bye to his other grandparents.

Charlie grabbed him in a big hug.

"Say good-bye," Roy said.

Charlie felt a lump in his throat. He couldn't cry. Sally had said, "No tears!" She didn't want to upset Roy.

"You be a good boy in California," he said. "Go to school. Learn to read and write. Then you can write Uncle Charlie a letter every day. Okay?"

Roy nodded. He hugged Charlie around the neck.

Outside, Mama, Alma, and Sally were hugging good-bye. Charlie didn't think he could stand it.

"You ready, son?" Daddy said, taking the mop from him.

Charlie nodded. He was afraid to speak. He put Roy in the front seat of Lee's pickup and handed him an open bottle of Coca-Cola.

"Hurray! Don't have a tired, thirsty face!" Roy said.

Lee rolled his eyes at Charlie, but smiled.

"I guess we'll hear that all the way to California, now."

Lee shook hands with Charlie and then hugged him. He got in beside Roy. He started the engine. It made a clunking and hissing sound. Charlie hoped the truck would make it all the way to California. It was such a long way.

Sally climbed in beside Roy and slammed the door. She leaned out to hug everyone one more time.

"I'll write you a long letter all about Roy and California," she said in Charlie's ear. "Don't worry. We'll come back next year when things are better." Charlie swallowed hard. He'd heard about next year before.

Lee pulled the truck onto the dirt road. Roy stood on the seat and looked out the rear window.

Charlie waved and tried to smile. He wanted to remember Roy's face always. He kept waving to him and Roy kept waving back.

The whole family stood in the road and waved until the dust swallowed up the truck.

Dust Storm!

Charlie moved uncomfortably in the hot truck. He was squashed between his father and the gear shift on one side, and his sister and mother on the other. The road was full of holes. His father kept having to slow down and shift gears.

"Mama, make Charlie sit still," Alma said. "I want to go to sleep."

Charlie stuck out his tongue at her. Alma hit him on the arm.

"That's enough, Alma," Mama said. Charlie wrinkled his nose at Alma.

"You too, Charlie," Mama said.

Daddy sighed and rubbed the back of his neck.

"This road is the last thing anyone fixes these days," he said. "But I sure wish they would fix it. My back would thank them."

"Want me to drive?" Mama asked.

"Let's switch the next time we stop for gas."

Outside, Charlie saw acres of brown fields. Houses were covered in dust.

Charlie knew times were hard. It had never seemed real until now. It was different since their luck had run out.

"It's getting darker," Alma said. "Are we almost there?"

"No," Mama said. She leaned her head back against the seat.

"I sure hope we aren't in for a shower," Daddy said. "This road will be one giant mud hole."

He reached out of the open window to fix the side mirror.

"Mercy," Daddy whispered.

"What is it?" Charlie asked.

"Dust storm!" Daddy said, pulling the car to the right. He stopped the engine.

Charlie didn't have to ask what that was. Walls of dust carried by the wind. Sometimes towns were in

16

total darkness for hours. Up to now, he had only heard stories about dust storms.

"Roll up the windows," Daddy said. "I'll get some blankets out of the back. Sometimes it gets as cold as winter during a storm."

They all got out and stood looking at the rolling, churning wall of gray. It looked endless. It went up and out forever on the horizon. Charlie thought the whole state of Oklahoma must be covered by the storm.

"Daddy, there's a house over there." Alma pointed. They looked toward a house that was leaning a bit to one side. It was buried in dust up to the windowsills.

"We'd be better off in there," Mama said.

Daddy nodded.

The family ran across the open field. The wind whipped at their clothes. As they reached the house, the door opened a small crack. A voice yelled at them to stop.

"Dust storm!" Daddy yelled above the sound of the wind.

The door opened wider. A wrinkled hand waved them in. Charlie could hardly see inside. Sunlight barely came through the dirty windows. There was just one room.

"I thought you was the sheriff coming to run us off again."

Charlie looked at the speaker. One of her front teeth was missing. She reminded Charlie of the women he

had seen standing beside the shacks near the city. A little girl about Roy's age held on to the woman's leg. She peeked shyly out from behind her mother.

"I stuffed up the cracks in the house during the last duster," the woman said. "The dust still gets in some. Do you have something you can wet and put over your faces?"

"Handkerchiefs," Mama said, pulling four clean ones out of her pocketbook. The woman pointed to a bucket of water beside the door.

The room got darker and darker. Charlie wondered if they really were better off in there. It sounded like a sleet storm hitting the house. It was still hot and the dust was starting to make Charlie's eyes water and his throat burn.

The little girl sat on a ragged blanket on the floor. She cried softly. The woman put her arm around her and held her close.

Charlie and his family sat down on their blankets in the middle of the floor. There was no furniture.

"Amy usually works herself into a state during one of these storms," the woman said.

Charlie looked at the little girl. Her tears were making muddy streaks down her cheeks. She wasn't so different from Roy, he thought. He got up and went to sit beside her.

"Hey, Amy," he said. "How about if you and me

lie down on this blanket? I'll play you a song on my harmonica."

The little girl looked at her mother, who nodded. Amy gave one last sniffle and lay down.

It was starting to get colder. Charlie covered himself and Amy with his blanket. He couldn't hold his handkerchief over his face while he played. He put it over his eyes and nose and put his harmonica to his mouth. Amy giggled.

He peeked out from under one corner of the handkerchief.

"What are you laughing at?" he teased.

She giggled again.

Charlie lay with his knees bent so he could tap his feet if he needed to. He started off playing "Arkansas Traveler." Then he played jigs and reels and hillbilly songs. He had heard the fiddle players perform them on the Grand Ole Opry radio show.

Amy clapped her hands and hummed along. Charlie sucked in dust sometimes and had to stop to cough. Amy always giggled and said, "More." Outside, the wind howled louder.

After a while, Amy closed her eyes, but Charlie kept playing.

The wind slowed and the room got brighter. Amy was still asleep when Charlie and his family said goodbye to the woman.

"I wish I could have said good-bye to Amy," Charlie said.

"I know," Mama said. "But it's best not to wake her."

As they climbed back into the truck, Charlie saw his warm bottle of Coca-Cola stuck in back of the seat.

He grabbed the bottle. He opened it with the opener on the dashboard.

"I'll be right back," he hollered over his shoulder.

"Did you forget something?" the woman asked from the doorway.

"Would you give this to Amy when she wakes up," Charlie said. "I just opened it. I'm sorry it's warm."

"What's your name?" the woman asked, taking it from him.

"Charlie," he answered. "Charlie Dodson."

"Well, Charlie Dodson," she said. "You have a good heart."

Back in the truck, Charlie thought about Roy. He hoped that somebody with a good heart in California would play music for him and give him Coca-Cola.

Sticking Together

"Are we almost there?" Charlie asked. He tried to stretch one leg out at a time.

"Almost," Daddy answered. He'd been saying that for hours.

"Doesn't any of this look familiar?" Mama asked.

Charlie shook his head.

"I don't know why it would," Daddy said. "It has been four years since we were here."

"That's true," Mama said. "And it does look different."

"Dustier," Alma said.

Charlie couldn't remember Daddy's parents very well. He wished that they could have gone to Mama's parents. He had seen them just last year. They drove up with some people who had money to buy gasoline.

Mama's parents were fat and smiling all the time. They brought Charlie a chocolate bar and loved his harmonica playing. But Charlie and his family couldn't live with them. Mama was one of ten kids. Three of them, with their families, had already moved home. Mama's parents didn't have any more room.

Daddy was an only child. His parents had plenty of room. All Charlie remembered about them was that they were thin and lived on a farm. He hoped they liked harmonica music.

Daddy turned the truck onto an even bumpier road. They passed a mailbox that said DODSON in big white letters. Charlie half stood to see over the dashboard.

A gray house came into view. As they got closer, Charlie could see that it used to be white, but the paint had peeled off down to the bare wood. The windmill for pumping water stood behind the house. Charlie tried to remember having seen the place before.

Daddy stopped the truck and shut off the engine. They all piled out and stood stretching in front of the house. Charlie could hear voices inside.

The screen door banged open. A thin man with gray hair, wearing overalls, stepped out onto the porch.

"So you finally made it," he said, smiling. "We've been looking for you all day. Grandma's worried herself to death."

As he came down the steps toward them, Grandma came out of the house. She was even thinner than the picture Charlie had seen of her. She had on a red-and-white checked apron. Her hair was piled on top of her head.

"Grandma, come and look at how these young ones have grown," Grandpa said. "I don't even know them."

"I don't expect they know you either, Grandpa," Grandma said, smiling at Charlie and Alma. "Come and give your grandma a hug."

Alma and Charlie hugged her. She smelled like cinnamon. They hugged Grandpa next.

"I hear you are the best harmonica player this side of the Mississippi," Grandpa said to Charlie.

Charlie felt his face get hot and looked down at his dusty shoes.

"Later I want you to play every song you know for me," Grandpa said.

"Outside," Grandma added. "My ears never could handle much noise."

Noise? Charlie thought. His harmonica playing

25

wasn't noise! He rolled his eyes at Alma. She shrugged. Did Grandma expect him to play his music outside, even in winter?

"Right now we're going to have some iced tea and one of three apple pies Grandma made just for you."

Charlie's mouth began to water. At least Grandma liked to cook, he thought.

"Heck," Grandpa said. "If you'd been just a few hours later, we would have had enough pies to last a month."

"Hush now, Grandpa," Grandma said.

Daddy laughed.

"Grandma cooks when she's worried," Grandpa whispered to Charlie.

"You don't need to worry about us anymore," Daddy said, hugging Grandma.

Later, with full stomachs, they sat on the front-porch steps. Charlie looked out over the land. The fields were an endless sea of brown. The trees that ringed the house were coated with dust. They also leaned toward the left side of the house. The front yard that was once a green lawn was now nothing but dirt.

"How are your folks getting along, Hazel?" Grandma asked Mama.

"Barely making it," Mama replied. "At last count, there were 15 living at home."

Grandma shook her head.

"Are they getting any help from the government?" she asked.

"The last letter I got said that they had gone to the Relief Office. They applied for a food allowance and a clothing allowance to buy shoes for the kids," Mama said. "The woman they talked to seemed to think the food allowance would be granted. It might take several months before they find out, though."

"Several months! A person could starve by then," Grandma said.

"President Roosevelt's New Deal has a few problems to work out yet," Daddy said.

"At least he's trying to help the people," Mama said.

Grandpa got up slowly from the steps and winked at Charlie.

"Who wants a tour of the vegetable garden?" he asked.

"I do," Charlie said. He was glad for a chance to walk around.

"Just the person I had in mind," Grandpa said. "I was hoping to get you to help me with the weeding and watering. We have to take good care of this garden if we want it to grow."

They walked around to the back of the house. There was a square of land fenced off with chicken wire.

"I only planted it a few weeks ago," Grandpa said.

"We've got carrots, potatoes, onions, tomatoes, corn, and strawberries."

Charlie got down on his hands and knees to get a better look. Here the earth was a richer, darker brown and smelled strong. Little shoots of real green were poking through the soil. It was beautiful.

"Weeding and watering is the easy part," Grandpa said. "It's the dust that might do it in. We haven't had a bad duster in a while, though."

"We were in a duster on the way here," Charlie said.

"Your daddy told me. Don't tell Grandma or we'll be up to our chins in apple pies!" Grandpa said.

Charlie grinned and nodded.

"Dusters are really bad here, aren't they?"

"Well, you haven't seen any as bad as the ones we get here," Grandpa said. "I watched the last duster from my bedroom window on the second floor. The dust was so thick you could cut it with a knife. You'll never guess what I saw right by the window."

"What?" Charlie asked. Grandpa looked like he was trying not to smile.

"A prairie dog trying to dig his burrow."

Charlie laughed.

"You've got to watch this guy and his stories," Daddy said, walking up.

"I never tell nothing but the truth," Grandpa said, putting his hand over his heart.

For a moment, nobody said anything. The only sound was the buzzing of grasshoppers out in the fields.

Then Daddy asked, "Do you think I might find a job in town?"

"Odd jobs, maybe, son," Grandpa answered. "A few of the stores in town might need some help. Everyone around here needs work. A lot of people have lost their farms. Those of us that haven't figure we will only get a few bushels of wheat this year. Selling it might not even cover the cost of cutting it." He looked out over the fields and sighed. "If only it would rain."

"It'll be okay. Next year will be better," Daddy said. He put an arm around Grandpa's shoulders. "At least we're together."

Grandpa pulled a handkerchief from his back pocket and blew his nose.

"You're right, son," he said. "There's always next year. As long as our family sticks together, we'll make it until then."

Charlie was worried. How were Sally and Lee and Roy going to make it? They were so far away from their family.

Hobos and Okies

Charlie wiped his forehead with the back of his hand. He bent over to fill his watering can again from the tap at the bottom of the water tank.

He worked in the garden every day, watering and weeding—and hoping. So far he'd planted the carrots twice. Then he spent two days clearing the dust away after the last dust storm.

He wanted to have hot buttered corn and strawberry shortcake by the Fourth of July. Grandpa said it might not work out. They might have to wait until next year to grow a good garden. Charlie didn't want to wait.

He ran up and down the rows with his watering can. He played scales on his harmonica as he went. He tried to sound like the train whistle he heard in the distance. Finally he just breathed through the harmonica, making funny sounds.

Grandma stepped out on the back porch. The smell of baking bread drifted out to the garden.

"Charlie, please," Grandma said. She sat down on the step. "Take that thing out of your mouth. My ears need a rest."

Charlie frowned at her. Her eyes were closed and she didn't see him. He shoved the harmonica deep into his pocket and dropped the empty watering can loudly by the steps. Grandma jumped at the sound, but she didn't open her eyes.

Near the front porch, Charlie picked up a stick and wrote his name in the dust. He wished he had someplace to go.

Daddy had a job delivering groceries in town. Mama spent days at the Baptist Church sorting used clothing. The clothes were boxed and sent to the people in the shack towns outside the city.

Alma usually went with Mama. On Saturdays, Alma worked at the Rexall Drugstore. Grandma worked at the church, too, sometimes. Grandpa was always having meetings with the other farmers. Charlie was tired of staying at home.

Charlie went inside and stood beside his parents' radio. He turned it on and off. He moved the dial to 650. On Saturday nights, he used to hear the Grand Ole Opry. Of course, nothing happened now. His grandparents didn't have electricity. They had gas lights and a windmill to pump the water. But they didn't have the most important thing, electricity.

He picked up *The Panhandle Herald* to see if there was anything interesting happening. There was a meeting in town about the terrible conditions in the area and what could be done about them. Charlie didn't think that was the thing for him.

There was the promise of a horse race at Texhoma's Fourth of July Rodeo. It sounded exciting, but it didn't help Charlie today.

There was a notice about Miss Olive Graham showing people how to can fruits and vegetables at home. Charlie put the paper down. He wasn't that desperate, yet.

Charlie sighed. He went back out on the front porch and sat down. He didn't know if he was bored enough to walk into town in the heat. Charlie shaded his eyes. He could just make out the form of someone coming up the road.

"Grandma!" Charlie called as he ran to the back of the house. "Someone's coming."

Grandpa came outside then.

"Another hobo getting off the train probably," he said.

"I sure do wish we didn't live so close to the tracks," Grandma said. "Send him on his way, Pa."

"You know I can't do that," Grandpa said.

Charlie knew that Grandma couldn't send a hobo away hungry either.

Grandpa walked to the front yard. A skinny kid about Alma's age walked up. A dirty cap was pulled down, low over his eyes.

"Do you want to work for some supper?" Grandpa asked.

The boy nodded.

"Tell you what, son," Grandpa said. "You wash the windows and I'll give you two meals. You can sleep in the barn tonight, too."

"Thank you, sir," the boy said.

Grandma shook her head.

"I swear we're going to have the cleanest windows in the county," she whispered to Charlie.

"Maybe that man two days ago missed a few spots," Charlie said.

Grandma chuckled.

"No doubt," she said.

"Charlie," Grandpa called. "Come show this young man where the buckets and rags are."

Charlie was glad to go. He hadn't talked to anyone

even near his own age, except Alma, since they left home.

"What's your name?" Charlie asked, as they walked to the barn.

"Jim," the boy said.

"Where are you going?"

"No place now."

"What does that mean?" Charlie asked.

"I was going to Oklahoma, but now I'm here."

"Where did you come from?"

"You sure do ask a lot of questions," Jim said. Charlie handed him a bucket. He could hear voices up by the house. Mama, Alma, and Daddy were coming home for lunch.

Jim sighed and picked up a handful of rags.

"I'm from Oklahoma," he said. "I went to California a year ago to pick peaches. I wanted to come back. So I did."

"Where are your parents?" Charlie asked.

"I ain't got none."

Jim pushed past Charlie and back out into the hot sunshine.

"I've got work to do now."

"My sister is in California," Charlie said. He followed Jim to the house. "We got a letter from her a while back. She said it's real pretty out there."

"It's pretty to look at," Jim said. "But they treat you bad."

"Who does?" Charlie asked. He couldn't imagine anyone treating Sally and Lee bad. And never Roy. Who wouldn't love Roy?

"The farmers, the store owners," Jim said. "They call anyone from Oklahoma an Okie. They say it like it's a bad word. If you're an Okie you have to sit in a special place in the movie theater. You can't even go in some of the cafes."

"That's not fair," Charlie said.

"They think just 'cause we're down on our luck we're criminals. They think you might steal from them—or worse."

"My sister wouldn't do anything bad," Charlie said, jamming his toe into the soft ground.

"You know that, but the people out there don't," Jim said. "If she has any sense, she'll come on back to Oklahoma where people will treat her right."

"What about little kids?" Charlie asked. "They treat kids okay, don't they?"

Jim stopped working and turned around. Charlie gritted his teeth as he waited for the answer.

"I don't know about real little kids," Jim said. "But I was in school for a while out there. One day, my teacher told me not to come back. She said I was just a dumb Okie. And I was never going to learn anything anyway."

"What did you do?" Charlie asked.

Jim shrugged. "I came back to Oklahoma," he said.

Charlie's head hurt. He suddenly wanted to lie down and not move.

"I'll see you later," he called to Jim. He ran up the back-porch steps.

Inside, he found everyone sitting around the kitchen table. The sandwiches that Grandma made sat untouched in the middle of the table. Daddy held a letter in his hand.

Charlie sat down next to Alma.

"We got a letter from Sally," she said.

Mama looked like she was about to cry.

"What did she say?" Charlie asked.

"They want to come home," Alma said.

Charlie jumped up.

"She's coming home? Roy's coming home! Hurray!"

Alma pulled him back down into his chair.

"It's not quite that easy," Daddy said. "Their truck doesn't work anymore and they don't have much money. Sally says they might just wait by the road until someone offers them a ride."

"Did she—" Charlie began. He took a deep breath. "Did she say why they want to come home?"

"She just said that things haven't worked out like they had hoped," Daddy said.

"And she's sick," Mama added. "She didn't even send us her address so we could help her." Mama wiped a tear away with one finger.

"Fruit pickers don't have a permanent address,"

Daddy said. "They move around all the time. Besides, they've got doctors there. Lee has enough sense to send us a telegram if they really need help."

Grandpa got up to swat a fly.

"The important thing is that they're coming home," Grandma said.

"I know you're right," Mama said. "But I'll worry just the same."

Charlie thought about what Jim had said. Should he tell his family? No, they were already worried enough. And Grandma was right. The important thing was they were coming home. No teacher was going to call Roy a dumb Okie.

Charlie smiled to himself. He imagined Roy helping him with the garden. He couldn't wait to see him dancing to harmonica music after supper again. It suddenly didn't matter if Grandma ever let Charlie play his music inside. He would play outside all winter and not mind, as long as Roy was there to listen.

Charlie ran back outside. He wanted to tell Jim that he wasn't the only Okie who had decided to come home.

Relief

Charlie lay on the sofa. He watched a fly buzz around his empty glass. He wasn't allowed to make any noise in the house today. Grandma had a headache. It was too hot to play outside.

It had been weeks since the letter from Sally. Everyone was in a bad mood from worrying about her—and about Daddy.

The grocery store had been sold to some new people from Tulsa. They said they couldn't afford to pay a delivery "boy." Daddy still went to town on his bicycle every day. Sometimes he found a job for a few hours. Mostly he came back with empty pockets.

Grandma and Grandpa still answered the door to hobos. They didn't give them nearly as much food as they did before, though.

Mama suggested that Daddy apply for relief. Boy, was there a fight over that. Charlie could still hear his parents.

"I'll be hanged if I'm going to ask anyone to give me anything," Daddy said. "We've always taken care of ourselves. We always will."

"We're going to need money for food soon," Mama said.

"I'll get a job," Daddy said.

"There aren't any jobs," Mama said.

"But asking for relief is like saying 'I give up. I quit.' I'll never do that."

"No one is asking you to give up," Mama said.

The screen door slammed. Daddy stomped out to the fields. Mama went after him.

Charlie didn't know what she said to him, but later they came back holding hands.

Alma still had her job. And Jim. Alma had fallen madly in love the minute she saw him. She talked Grandpa into finding him more jobs. Grandma was still feeding him. He was still sleeping in the barn, too.

Charlie thought it was great at first. He liked talking

to Jim. But lately, Jim was talking more and more to Alma instead. Every time Charlie came around them, Alma gave him her "go away" look.

The hot summer days seemed to drag by. Charlie was so bored he even started wishing school would start.

To save money, the school in town had been let out early for summer vacation. It wouldn't start again until late October. Even then, Charlie didn't know if he'd get to go. His parents would have to have money to pay for his books and supplies.

Alma was saving her money from work. She would get to go to school.

"I wish I could get a job," Charlie said.

"You've got a job," Grandpa said. "And I don't think you've done it yet today."

Charlie got up. Grandpa was right. The garden hadn't been watered yet.

"I mean a paying job," Charlie said. Grandpa followed him through the kitchen and out the back door.

"Just wait till you taste this stuff," Grandpa said. "Then you'll feel rich."

"How dumb," Charlie said to himself.

The garden just made Charlie angry. He wanted it to be a success. The last duster buried it. Then rabbits and grasshoppers ate half of the corn.

"Do you really think this is going to ever work, Grandpa?" Charlie asked.

Grandpa looked at him a long time before he finally spoke.

"I don't know," he said. "But we can't give up trying."

Charlie wanted to give up.

"Next year when it rains," Grandpa said, "you won't know this place, Charlie. Your garden will be a jungle. And there will be beautiful golden wheat growing taller than you."

Charlie wondered if Grandpa really thought it would be better next year.

Grandpa turned from the fields. He shaded his eyes to look out toward the road.

"Oh, no," he said.

"What?" Charlie asked.

"Hobos again," Grandpa said.

"They must tell each other where they can find people with good hearts," Charlie said.

"People with no sense, you mean," Grandpa said. "We can't keep feeding these men and us, too."

"It's so hot, I don't feel much like eating," Charlie said. "They can have mine."

Grandpa shook his head.

"You don't eat enough as it is," he said. "Besides, one of them looks big enough to eat us out of house and home."

Charlie walked up a row of corn with his watering can. He stood beside Grandpa and shaded his eyes.

As he watched, the fat one set something down on the road. The something got up and started running. It was a child.

Charlie started walking slowly at first, then faster. Grandpa came with him.

"Charlie! Charlie!" a voice called. It was Roy!

Charlie broke into a run then. He caught Roy up in his arms. They spun around and around. It seemed as though they had never been apart.

Charlie hugged Sally and then Lee and then Sally again. The rest of the family joined them now in the hugging and laughing and crying.

"How did you get here?" Mama asked.

"Some man brought us all the way from California," Lee said. "Can you believe it?"

"Thank the Lord there are still some good people left in the world," Grandma said.

"He brought all our things, too," Sally said. "We left them out on the main road. We'll have to get them later."

"I hope you got his address so we can thank him properly," Grandpa said.

"He wouldn't give it to me," Sally said. "He said if we would just help somebody else that would be thanks enough."

"People like that give me hope," Mama said.

"Let's don't stand out here in the hot sun all day," Grandma said. "Sally needs to sit down."

Inside, Grandma poured glasses of tea while everyone sat down in the living room. She brought out a loaf of bread and a jar of strawberry jam.

Charlie held Roy on his lap. Sally ate piece after piece of bread smeared with jam. Her stomach stuck out in front. Her dress looked like the buttons were going to pop off. The food must have been good in California, Charlie thought.

"Glad to see there was a reason you were sick," Mama said, patting Sally's knee. Sally smiled and glanced up at Lee. Lee smiled, too.

"Yeah," he said. "She's not sick anymore. Just hungry all the time. I swear she could eat 24 hours a day."

Sally laughed and reached for another slice of bread.

"I'm eating for two now," she said.

"Just as long as you don't go on eating for two after the baby gets here," Lee said.

Charlie felt his face redden. He felt stupid. Why hadn't he realized before that his sister was pregnant?

Daddy had been very quiet. Finally he spoke.

"When is the baby due?" he asked.

"Not for three or four months," Sally said.

Daddy sighed. He stretched out his long legs.

"I guess I'll go into town to the Relief Office before it closes," he said, getting up.

Charlie thought Daddy looked really tired.

"Maybe I can get us a food allowance, at least," he

said. He smiled weakly at Sally and patted her head. "I think we might need it."

"Oh, Daddy," she said. She stood up to hug him. "I'm sorry to be so much trouble."

"It's okay, honey," he said.

That evening, Charlie sat on the front porch listening to the crickets. He was waiting for Daddy.

It was long past supper. The dishes were washed. Roy had been asleep for hours. Alma came out with Jim and they sat beside Charlie.

"Don't you want to play a song?" Jim asked.

"Naw," Charlie said.

"What's wrong?" Alma asked.

"How come Daddy's not home?" he asked.

Alma shrugged.

"Maybe he found a job for a few hours," she said.

"Maybe, or . . ." Charlie swallowed hard. "Maybe he walked to town and just kept on walking. It would sure be easier to live without a family to look after."

"Your pa wouldn't do that," Jim said.

"Of course not," Alma said angrily. "You know that."

Charlie did know it. All the same, he'd feel better when Daddy was back.

Out of the darkness came the sound of happy whistling. Pretty soon, the gate swung open and Daddy was in the front yard.

"Ah, the welcoming committee," Daddy said.

Charlie and Alma ran to hug him on either side.

"Come on," Daddy said, hugging them back. "I've only been gone a few hours."

"Did you apply for relief?" Charlie asked.

Daddy was quiet a minute. He looked up at the stars.

"I almost didn't," he said. "I walked up to that door four times before I walked inside."

"What did they say?" Alma said.

"They thought we could get a food allowance," Daddy said. "But it will be a while before it comes through."

"Where were you?" Charlie asked.

"Fixing typewriters," Daddy said. "I repaired one in the Relief Office tonight. I'm going back tomorrow to clean their other machines."

"Lucky you went in," Charlie said.

"You're right, Charlie Boy," Daddy said. "And we're lucky our family is all together again."

"Amen to that," Mama said, coming out on the porch.

Charlie took out his harmonica and started polishing it on his shirt. He smiled. Their luck hadn't really run out when Daddy lost his job. When your luck ran out, you ended up like those hobos singing for dimes in the city. Or worse, like the father of Alma's friend who jumped off the building.

Jim was luckier than most hobos, because he had found Charlie's family. Charlie's family was lucky because they had each other. And they always had next year. It was bound to be better.

ABOUT THIS BOOK

The Great Depression started in 1929. By 1933, when this story takes place, there were about 123 million people in the United States. Almost 13 million were out of work.

In 1992 there were about 250 million people in the United States with about 9 million out of work. People say that times are hard now, but the Great Depression was even worse.

It began when the market for stocks and bonds crashed. Stocks and bonds are agreements people make to borrow and invest money. Owning stocks is like being a partner in a business. Stocks give you the right to a share of the money the business earns.

Owning bonds is like putting money in the bank. You allow the business to use your money, and they in turn pay you for the use of your money.

If businesses do not make a profit, the people who own stock have nothing to share. Also, the people

53

who own bonds will not receive the payments promised to them.

Even worse, if businesses are not expected to make profits in the future, the stocks and bonds may become worthless. The money invested in them may be lost.

This is what happened on October 24, 1929. People suddenly became very unsure of whether businesses could earn profits. The prices of stocks and bonds fell a lot. Some became totally worthless. And the people who had invested in those stocks and bonds lost their money. Some people were so upset about their losses that they killed themselves.

The disaster did not end on one day. Like the dominoes Charlie imagined, the stock market crash affected everyone. As more businesses across the country failed, more people lost their jobs and homes.

The people in Oklahoma and in other surrounding states were hit hardest. Besides businesses failing, there wasn't enough rain. Nothing would grow on the farms. The area became known as the Dust Bowl.

President Franklin Roosevelt tried to help the people by using government money for food. He also started programs to create jobs for people willing to work. Still, the times did not really get better until the United States became involved in World War II in 1941. The Great Depression lasted twelve long years.

N.A.